ROMANCES OF OLD FRANCE

ROMANCES

OF

OLD FRANCE

BY

RICHARD Le GALLIENNE

Short Story Index Reprint Series

BOOKS FOR LIBRARIES PRESS

FREEPORT, NEW YORK

First Published 1905
Reprinted 1969

STANDARD BOOK NUMBER:
8369-3023-1

LIBRARY OF CONGRESS CATALOG CARD NUMBER:
75-81271

MANUFACTURED
BY
HALLMARK LITHOGRAPHERS, INC.
IN THE U.S.A.

To my friend

JAMES CARLTON YOUNG

The writer desires to thank Mr.
John Brisben Walker *for his
kindness in allowing the reproduc-
tion of four of the following stories
which originally appeared in* The
Cosmopolitan.

CONTENTS

KING FLORUS
AND THE FAIR JEHANE

ROMANCES OF OLD FRANCE

&

I. King Florus and the Fair Jehane

THE prettiest story, except, perhaps, "Aucassin and Nicolete," of those which such lovers of old French literature as Mr. Lang and William Morris have rediscovered for us is the "Tale of King Florus and the Fair Jehane." Also, it comes to us in its English dress with the advantage of having been translated by William Morris. It is one of the happiest, least mannered, of his translations.

With its central incident we have all been familiar since we read "Cymbeline" —the wager about a wife's honor. Shakespeare, of course, found his motive in Boccaccio, who again found it somewhere in folk-literature, in which all over the world it is of common occurrence.

The story really ought to be called the "Tale of Squire Robin and the Fair Jehane"—for King Florus is brought in for little more than decoration. The old mediæval romancers were great snobs. No doubt they had to be. They depended for their livelihood upon the fashionable, moneyed class, called in those days "the great" and in later times "the quality." No one under the degree of a knight could be permitted to love within their high-bred pages. So the author of "King Florus and the Fair Jehane" evidently felt that the loves of a high-born lady and a simple squire, however beau-

tiful and humanly touching, needed
to be set in a gilded frame of roy-
alty to make the picture accepta-
ble to eyes polite. The picture
could be taken out of the frame,
with the greatest ease, and the real
story remain complete.

King Florus, indeed, has hardly
more to do with it than the conventional "Prince" in the envoy of
a ballad has to do with the ballad.
It is apparent that in his heart the
old romancer cared little for kings
and princes, for, after telling us in
perfunctory, formal fashion that
there was once a king who "had
to name King Florus of Ausay,"
married to the daughter of the
Prince of Brabant—both happy,
God-fearing young people, who
governed well and led useful lives

[13]

—he, with undisguised eagerness, leaves them at once to tell of "a knight who dwelt in the marches of Flanders and Hainault."

Now this knight "had to wife a full fair dame of whom he had a much fair daughter, who had to name Jehane and was then of the age of twelve years. Much word was there of this fair maiden; for in all the land was none so fair." As Jehane was now twelve years old, her mother was naturally anxious to have her married, and she was forever "admonishing" her husband on the subject; but he was so taken up with "tournays" that he gave it but little thought.

However, one day as he rode away from tourney with his valiant and well-beloved Squire Robin, he gave the subject serious attention. Robin, it must be said, had, quite innocently, promised his lord's wife to recall the matter to the knight's mind. The knight had done so well at the tourney, borne off "the praise and the prize"—"by means of the good deeds of Robin, his squire"—that he was in an accessible mood. The romancer gives us no hint that Robin had any ulterior motive when he impressed upon his lord that it was high time he should betroth his daughter. The outcome of his importunity seems to have been as little foreseen by him as by the reader. The romancer never speaks of the knight by name, but he has succeeded in making him live for us as a singularly attractive, simple, honest, warm-hearted man— a man whom one can imagine going on "tournays" if for no other reason than to escape the "polite" atmosphere of his wife's drawing-room. The conversation between him and his squire deserves to be read in its entirety, it gives the man so well: "'Robin, thou and thy lady give me no peace about the marrying of my daughter; but as yet I know and see no man in my land unto whom I would give her.' 'Ah, sir,' said Robin, 'there is not a knight in thy land who would not take her with a good will.' 'Fair friend Robin, they are of no avail, all of them; and forsooth to no one would I give her, save to one man only, and he forsooth is no knight.' 'Sir, tell me of him,' said Robin, 'and I shall speak to him so subtly that the marriage shall be made.' 'Certes, Robin, thou hast served me exceedingly well, and I have found thee a valiant man, and a loyal, and such as I be thou hast made

[16]

me, and great gain have I gotten by thee, to wit, five hundred pounds of land; for it was but a little while that I had but five hundred, and now have I a thousand, and I tell thee that I owe much to thee: wherefore will I give my fair daughter unto thee, if thou wilt take her.' 'Ha, sir,' said Robin, 'God's mercy, what is this thou sayest? I am too poor a person to have so high a maiden, nor one so fair and so rich as my damsel is; I am not meet thereto. For there is no knight in this land, be he never so gentle a man, but would take her with a good will.' 'Robin, know that no knight of this land shall have her, but I shall give her to thee, if thou will it; and thereto will I give thee four hun-

dred pounds of my land.' 'Ha, sir,' said
Robin, 'I deem that thou mockest me.'
'Robin,' said the knight, 'wot thou surely
that I mock thee not.' 'Ha, sir, neither
my lady nor her great lineage will accord
hereto.' 'Robin,' said the knight, 'naught
shall be done herein at the will of any of
them. Hold! here is my glove, I invest
thee with four hundred pounds of my
land, and I will be thy warrant for all.'
'Sir,' said Robin, 'I will naught nay-say
it; fair is the gift since I know that is
soothfast.' 'Robin,' said the knight,
'now hast thou the rights thereof.' Then
the knight delivered to him his glove, and
invested him with the land and his fair
daughter.''

But, as may be imagined, this disposal
of her daughter's hand was little to the
taste of the ambitious and elegant mother.
She calls her family together—''her broth-

ers, and her nephews and her cousins germain"—and they plead with the knight. He acts with his usual common sense. There are many rich men among them, he says: will any one of them give her four hundred pounds of land? If so, he will give her elsewhere.

"A-God's name," is their answer, "we be naught fain to lay down so much."

"Well, then," said the knight, "since ye will not do this, then suffer me to do with my daughter as I list."

"Sir, with a good will," said they.

Thereupon the knight made a knight of Squire Robin, and Robin and Jehane were wedded next day.

And here the tale begins. Robin had made a vow to visit the shrine of St. James the day after his knighting—whatever that day should be. It chanced to be his marriage-day, but none the less Robin was firm on his vow, in spite of criticism. Every one, including his old master and friend, took it ill of him. Yet his determination remained unshaken. Among others who mocked him was a certain Sir Raoul, a black-hearted knight who offered to bet four hundred pounds of land that he would win away the Fair Jehane's love before Sir Robin's return. Sir Robin takes the bet gayly, and takes the road for "Saint Jakem."

Now, while Sir Robin is away, Sir Raoul tries every means in his power to win his wager, but in vain. Finally, a few days before Sir Robin's return, by the treachery of her waiting-maid, he surprises Jehane as she is taking the rare bath of the Middle Ages, and

descries a mole upon her right
thigh. The reader will here, of
course, recall "Cymbeline."

On Sir Robin's return, Sir Raoul
boldly claims the forfeit, and, for
token that he has really won his
wager, he imparts to Sir Robin the
information thus foully obtained.

Sir Robin on the morrow pays his
forfeit to Sir Raoul, and rides away
once more, sad of heart, to Paris.
But he is hardly on the road before
Jehane is after him. Here the old
romancer tells his story so charmingly that it is sacrilege to attempt
to retell it.

"On the first hour of the night,"
we read, "the lady arose, and took
all pennies that she had in her cof-
fer, and took a nag and a harness
thereto, and gat her to the road;

[21]

and she had let shear her fair tresses, and was otherwise arrayed like to an esquire. So much she went by her journeys that she presently came to Paris, and went after her lord; and she said and declared that she would never make an end before she found him. Thus she rode like to a squire. And on a morning she went forth out of Paris, and wended the way toward Orleans until she came to the Tomb Isory, and there she fell in with her lord, Sir Robin. Full fain she was when she saw him, and she drew up to him and greeted him, and he gave her greeting back and said: 'Fair friend, God give thee joy!' 'Sir,' said she, 'whence art thou?' 'Forsooth, fair friend, I am of old Hainault.' 'Sir, whither wendest thou?' 'Forsooth, fair friend, I wot not right well whither I I go, nor where I shall dwell. Forsooth, needs must I where fortune shall lead me;

and she is contrary enough; for I have lost the thing in the world that most I ever loved; and she also hath lost me. Withal I have lost my land, which was great and fair enough. But what hast thou to name, whither doth God lead thee?' 'Certes, sir,' said Jehane, 'I am minded for Marseilles on the sea, where is war as I hope. There would I serve some valiant man, about whom I shall learn me arms if God will. For I am so undone in mine own country that therein for a while of time I may not have peace. But, sir, meseemeth that thou be a knight, and I would serve thee with a right good will if it please thee. And of my company wilt thou be naught worsened.' 'Fair friend,' said Sir Robin, 'a knight am I verily. And where I may look to find war, thitherward would I draw full willingly. But tell me what thou hast to name?' 'Sir,' said she,

'I have to name John.' 'In a good hour,' quoth the knight. 'And thou, sir, how hight thou?' 'John,' said he, 'I have to name Robin.' 'Sir Robin, retain me as thine esquire, and I will serve thee to my power.' 'John, so would I with a good will. But so little of money have I that I must needs sell my horse before three days are worn. Wherefore I wot not how to do to retain thee.' 'Sir,' said John, 'be not dismayed thereof, for God will aid thee if it please him. But tell me where thou wilt eat thy dinner?' 'John, my dinner will soon be made; for not another penny have I than three sols of Paris.' 'Sir,' said John, 'be naught dismayed thereof, for I have hard on ten pounds Tour-

nais, whereof thou shalt not lack.'
'Fair friend John, hast thou mickle thanks.'

"Then made they good speed to Montlhéry: there John dight meat for his lord and they ate. When they had eaten, the knight slept in a bed and John at his feet. When they had slept, John did on the bridles, and they mounted and gat to the road."

But, alas! nobody wanted soldiers in Marseilles, and, as it was palpably impossible for a newly made knight to do anything else but fight, there seemed nothing for Sir Robin or his Squire John to do but presently starve.

But here Squire John's accomplishments as a woman come

charmingly to the rescue; he makes this proposal:

"'Sir,' said John, 'I have yet well an hundred sols of Tournay, and if it please thee, I will sell our two horses, and make money thereby: for I am the best of bakers that ye may wot of; and I will make French bread, and I doubt me not but I shall earn my spending well and bountifully.' 'John,' said Sir Robin, 'I grant it thee to do all as thou wilt.'

"So on the morrow John sold the two horses and bought corn and let grind it, and fell to making French bread so good that he sold it for more than the best baker of the town might do; and he did so much within two years that he had well an hundred pounds of chattels."

Can one ever eat French bread again without thinking of Sir Robin and his faithful squire?

The fairy bakery continued so successful that the ambitious Squire John designs to open a hostel. "I rede thee well," he says to Sir Robin, "that we buy us a very great house, and take to harboring good folk."

Sir Robin agrees with the condescending grace of a born aristocrat. Things went so well with Squire John's loyal industry that "Sir Robin had his palfrey, and went to eat and drink with the most worthy of the town, and John sent him wine and victual so all they that haunted his company marvelled thereat."

So five years went by, and all this time Sir Robin had never recognized his wife in the faithful squire. Nor did Sir Raoul recognize her either, passing through Marseilles and inevitably putting up at Squire John's hotel on his way to penitential pilgrimage through the Holy Land.

Sir Raoul's priest had imposed
this penance upon him, and he
had promised that on his return
he would make confession of h
crime and restitution of his wrong-
fully gotten lands. All this he
confides unsuspectingly to Squire
John.

After a while Squire John works
on his master to bring about his
return to his own country. Seven
years have they been in Marseilles,
and grown rich. But Sir Robin
hesitates. Squire John reassures
him, and adds, "Doubt thou nothing, for in all places, if it please
God, I shall earn enough for thee
and for me." At last Sir Robin
consents.

Now when Sir Robin and Squire
John arrived in their own coun-

try, they found that Sir Raoul had
repented him of his pious impulse
to confession and that he still
held Sir Robin's lands. Sir Robin
thereon challenges him to battle,
and does so mightily against him
that Sir Raoul begs for his mercy
—and, that being granted him,
goes overseas and so out of the
story. Sir Robin's victory, however, seems but a barren one for
him, for his wife is gone no man
knows whither, and his faithful
squire has not been seen for a
fortnight. Both, however, are all
this time comfortably hidden in
the boudoir of a friendly cousin of
the Fair Jehane, engaged in making "four pair of gowns"—"of
Scarlet, of Vair, of Perse, and of
cloth of silk"—and in nursing the

womanly beauty which had no doubt lost a little of its bloom and delicacy in the disguise of Squire John.

When Jehane is adjudged to be once more her fair self, she is revealed duly to her husband. So great was their joy at meeting again that they embraced together "for the space of the running of two acres or ever they might sunder."

And very soon after, Squire John is also restored to the lord he has so faithfully served.

"Thus," as the old romancer charmingly says, "were these two good persons together."

There, properly, the story ends; but beauty and virtue such as the Fair Jehane's cannot be finally rewarded by anything short of a royal marriage. So, after many years of happiness, Jehane is left a widow, and is in due time sought in marriage by King Florus, who, all this long while, has been vainly hoping for an heir to his kingdom. His first loved wife, of whom mention was made at the beginning of the story, has, at the instance of his disappointed subjects, been placed in a nunnery; and a second wife has died leaving him still childless.

In his widowerhood, friends bring him report of the beauty and wisdom of the Fair Widow Jehane, and at length he sets out to sue for her hand. This she gives him with appropriate ceremonies—and this time the prayers of King Florus were answered: for of their union were born a daughter who had to name Floria and a son who had to name Florence. This Florence in after days became so famous for feats of arms that "he was chosen to be Emperor of Constantinople;" while the daughter Floria "became queen of

the land of her father, and the son
of the King of Hungary took her
to wife, and lady she was of two
realms."

So, you see, we take leave of the
Fair Jehane in the very finest company. But, after all, one likes to
think of her best in that little
French bakery at Marseilles. Was
there ever a prettier fairy-tale of
the devotion of woman?

AMIS AND AMILE

II

Amis and Amile

"LA vie des saints martyrs Amis et
Amile" is, par excellence, the
fairy-tale of friendship. Greater love than
this hath no man—that he giveth his life
for his friend. Yet Amile did even more
than that, carried the ideal of renuncia-
tory comradeship to a symbolic extreme,
which in actual life, as in the story, could
be justified only by the certainty of a
miracle.

The love of Amis and Amile began with
life, as it was ended—or maybe merely
seemed to end—only with death. Long
ago, in that sufficiently legendary period
of human history distinguished by the

story-teller as "in the time of Pe-
pin, King of France," a child was
born in "the Castle of Bericain,"
"of a noble father of Alemaine,
who was of great holiness." The
pious parents vowed to God—
"and Saint Peter and Saint Paul"
—that they would carry their child
to Rome for baptism. Now about
the same time, in the castle of "a
Count of Alverne," similar, indeed identical, things were happening. The Count of Alverne
also was happy in a new-born son,
and—assisted by a heavenly vision
—he, too, decided to take his child
to Rome for baptism. But on the
same pilgrimage, the two parents,
hitherto unknown to each other,
met at Lucca; "and when they
found themselves to be of one pur-

pose, they joined company in all friendliness and entered Rome together. And the two children fell to loving one another so sorely that one would not eat without the other, they lived of one victual, and lay in one bed."

So the friendship of Amis and Amile began in their cradles, and that there should be no mistaking that they were born for each other, Nature, who predestines for us all, had made them so alike in person and character that it was impossible to tell one from the other. As a further symbol of their unity, the "Apostle of Rome" at their baptism—when "many a knight of Rome held them at the font with mickle joy, and raised them aloft even as God would"—gave to each

of them a cup (a "hanap") wrought of
wood, bound with gold and set with precious stones; the two cups being identical
as the two children. Then parents and
children "betook them thence home in
all joyance," and we hear no more of
them till Amis is thirty years old, with
his father upon his deathbed. The old
knight of Bericain thus addresses the son
he must leave behind, and wiser or more
beautiful advice has seldom come from
the dying. Here are his words: "Fair
son, well beloved, it behooveth me presently to die, and thou shalt abide and be
thine own master. Now firstly, fair son,
keep thou the commandments of God;
the chivalry of Jesus Christ do thou.
Keep thou faith to thy lords, and give aid
to thy fellows and friends. Defend the
widows and orphans. Uphold the poor
and needy: and all days hold thy last

day in memory. Forget not the fellowship and friendship of the son of the
Count of Alverne, whereas the Apostle of
Rome on one day baptized you both, and
with one gift honored you. Ye be alike
of beauty, of fashion, and stature, and
whoso should see you would deem you
to be brethren."

So the father died, but the son proved
too gentle and Christian of nature to
hold his own against the enemies that
now rose up against him. Always Amis
turned the other cheek, and so it fell that
he was despoiled of his heritage. In his
trouble he bethinks him of his old friend
and fellow. "Go we now," he says, "to
the Court of the Count Amile, who was
my friend and my fellow. Mayhappen
he will make us rich with his goods and
his havings."

However, on arriving at Amile's castle, they find that Amile is away—gone to comfort Amis for the death of his father. So the friends miss each other, and for two years and more Amile seeks Amis, and Amis Amile, "in France and in Alemaine." Meanwhile, Amis incidentally takes a wife, his bride's father having heard so well of him that he endows him and his company with gold and silver and "havings." Thus Amis and his "ten fellows" abide in comfort for a year and a half, Amile meanwhile having sought his friend "without ceasing." One cannot but note that while both friends no doubt love equally, Amile is the friend who does most throughout the story.

Amis and Amile

At the end of the year and a half, the conscience of Amis smites him. "We have done amiss," he says, "in that we have left seeking of Amile." So Amis and his knights set out toward Paris, and after various adventures are sitting at meat "by the water of Seine in a flowery meadow," when a company of French knights fall upon them. The day is going hard with them, when Amis cries out, "Who are ye, knights, who have will to slay Amis the exile and his fellows?"

"At that voice," says the storyteller, "Amile knew Amis his fellow and said: 'O thou Amis most well beloved, rest from my travail, I am Amile, son of the Count of Alverne, who have

[41]

not ceased to seek thee for two whole years.'"

The friends thereon embraced and, swearing "friendship and fellowship perpetual," betook them to the Court of Charles, King of France, where they became at once favorites of the King, Amis becoming treasurer, and Amile "server." "There might men behold them young, well attempered, wise, fair, and of like fashion and visage, loved of all and honored."

So abode they in happiness and prosperity for three years, at the end of which time it suddenly occurred to Amis that he was married and had not seen his wife for three years! "Fair sweet fellow," says he to his friend, "I desire sore to go see my wife whom I have left behind; and I will return the soonest that I may; and do thou abide at the Court." To this

Amis adds a word of advice: that Amile
should keep away from the King's daughter and that he should above all things
beware of "Arderi the felon." Now, as
might perhaps be expected, Amis has no
sooner departed than Amile forgets his
commandment and teaching, and—re-
members the King's daughter; "whereas," adds the monkish story-teller, "he
was no holier than David nor wiser than
Solomon."

Now comes "Arderi the felon" with a
false tale against Amis, which his friend
apparently believes—namely, that Amis
has stolen from the King's treasury and
is therefore fled away. Thereon, for
some unexplained reason, Amile swears
fealty and friendship with Arderi, and
unbosoms himself concerning the King's
daughter. Arderi reveals the secret to the
King. Amile denies the charge and chal-

lenges Arderi to the ordeal by battle.

Meanwhile, before the day appointed, Amile meets Amis by chance and tells him what has befallen. "Then said Amis, sighing: 'Leave we here our folk, and enter into this wood to lay bare our secret.' And Amis fell to blaming Amile, and said: 'Change we our garments and our horses, and get thee to my house, and I will do battle for thee against the traitor.'" The point, of course, of the change was that divine justice was supposed to preside over such duels as Amile had undertaken, and, as he was fighting for a lie, he must logically expect to fall in battle. With Amis in his place, justice might perhaps be hood-

winked. So man has thought to deceive the justice of heaven in all ages. The friends part from each other weeping, Amis making his way to the court in the semblance of Amile, and Amile going to his friend's house in the semblance of Amis—not, however, without a word of warning which one might have deemed unnecessary between such good friends. Thus, after the manner of Sigurd, Amile placed his sword between him and the wife of Amis; though Amis had so little confidence either in his friend or in his wife that, we read, "he betook himself," o' nights, "in disguise to his house to wot if Amile kept faith with him of his wife."

But this time Amile acquitted
[45]

himself better than either David or Solomon, and justified the faith of his friend.

Presently comes the day of battle. The false Arderi is duly vanquished, his head smitten off, and Amis rewarded with Belisaut the King's daughter, whom he honorably transfers to his friend. So Amile's affairs prosper, and it is soon time for Amis to be in trouble once more. Heaven, chastening whom it loveth—as the pious chronicler remarks—sends upon Amis the scourge of leprosy. He becomes so "mesel" that his wife hates him and endeavors ofttimes to strangle him. In this sore trouble, the heart of Amis turns again to his friend.

But when he reaches the Castle of Bericain, Amile's folk do not recognize Amis, and, seeing only an unclean leper, beat him sore and drive him and his company away. Thence he turns to Rome, where

he is hospitably entertained by the Holy
Father till a famine falls upon the land,
a famine so great "that the father had
will to thrust the son away from his
house." In this extremity Amis is borne
once more to the city of the Count Amile.

But by this time fortune had done its
worst. So soon as his servants sounded
the rattles (or clappers—"tartarelles")
by which lepers in the Middle Ages gave
sign of their approach, Amile, hearing the
sound, sent out one of his servants with
food for the sick man, and with it his own
birthcup filled with wine. As yet he had
no knowledge that the leper was Amis,
but when his servant returned he told
how the sick man had a "hanap" exactly
like his master's; and so Amis became
known again to Amile and by him and his
wife was welcomed lovingly to the castle,
leper though he was.

[47]

But the supreme test of Amile's love for Amis was yet to come. One night as the two friends were sleeping in the same room, the angel Raphael appeared to Amis and bade him tell Amile that if he were to slay his two children and wash Amis in their blood, his friend would be healed. Amile is awakened by the speech of the angel, and bids Amis reveal what he has heard. Sorely against his will, Amis delivers the divine message, and in much tribulation of soul Amile ponders it. At length, however, his sense of duty toward his friend triumphs over his love for his children, and he girds himself to make even this terrible sacrifice. And here let the old romancer take up the tale in his simple,

[48]

direct fashion: "Then Amile fell
to weeping privily and thinking
in his heart: 'This man forsooth
was apparelled before the King to
die for me, and why should I not
slay my children for him; if he
hath kept faith with me to the
death, why keep I not faith?' . . .

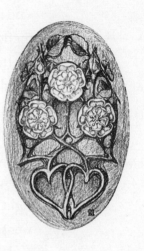

"Then the Count took his sword,
and went to the bed where lay his
children, and found them sleeping,
and he threw himself upon them,
and fell to weeping bitterly and
said: 'Who hath heard ever of a
father who of his own will hath
slain his child? Ah, alas, my children! I shall be no more your father, but your cruel murderer!' . .

"When he had so said, he cut
off their heads, and then laid them
behind the bed, and laid the heads

[49]

to the bodies, and covered them over even as they slept. And with their blood which he received, he washed his fellow, and said: 'Sire God, Jesus Christ, who commandest men to keep faith upon the earth, and who cleansest the mesel by thy word, deign thou to cleanse my fellow, for the love of whom I have shed the blood of my children.'

"Then was Amis cleansed of his meselry. And Amile clad him in his own right goodly raiment; and therewith they went to the church to give thanks there, and the bells by the grace of God rang of themselves. And when the people of the city heard that, they ran all together toward that marvel. . . .

"Now was come the hour of tierce, and neither the father nor the mother was yet entered in to their children; but the father sighed grievously for the death of his

babes. Then the Countess asked for her
children to make her joy, and the Count
said: 'Dame, let be, let the children
sleep!'

"Therewith he entered all alone to the
children to weep over them, and found
them playing in the bed; but the scars of
their wounds showed about the necks of
each of them even as a red fillet.

"Then he took them in his arms, and
bore them to their mother, and said:
'Make great joy, dame, whereas thy sons
whom I had slain by the commandment
of the Angel are alive again, and by their
blood is Amis cured and healed.'

"And when the Countess heard it she
said: 'O thou, Count, why didst thou not
lead me with thee to receive the blood of
my children, and I would have washed
therewith Amis thy fellow and my
Lord?'"

[51]

Nor must it be forgotten that on the self-same day that Amis was made whole, the devils bore off his inhuman wife; "they brake the neck of her, and bore away her soul."

So the love of Amis and Amile endured through life, and in their death they were not divided, for not only did they fall in battle together fighting for King Charles against the Lombards, but heaven itself set this final seal of miracle upon their love. On the field of Mortara where they fell, the King built two churches, dedicating one to St. Eusebius and the other to St. Peter. In one church was buried Amis and in the other Amile: "but on the morrow's morn the body of Amile, and his coffin

[52]

therewith, was found in the church of St. Eusebius hard by the coffin of Amis his fellow." Thus it came about that till the end of the seventeenth century the names of the two friends were to be found side by side in the calendar of saints and martyrs.

So Holy Church blesses a human love and hallows it.

The story of Amis and Amile is one well known in many forms to folklorists. It is to be met with in many languages, and learned authorities differ as to its origin. Some claim that it came from the East and some from Greece, and some that it is founded on actual historic incidents of the wars of Charlemagne. Mr. Joseph Jacobs (in his introduction to Will-

iam Morris's translation—"Old French Romances," Scribner's Sons) points out that the names of the heroes are clearly Latin—Amicus and Æmilius; and also refers to the fantastic conjecture that the proverb, "A miss is as good as a mile," has its explanation in this old story. Those who seek learning on the subject may find it in Mr. Jacobs's introduction above referred to, and by him be introduced to other authorities. Walter Pater's essay on "Two Early French Stories" in his volume on the Renaissance was probably the first introduction of the story to most English readers, William Morris following with the translation from which I have quoted. The original may be found in that pretty series the *Bibliothèque Elzevirienne*, and the ecclesiastical legend of the two friends in the *Acta Sanctorum*.

The charm of the romance is mainly in the story itself, and but little in its form, which is often crude and merely quaint, and seldom interesting from a dramatic or literary point of view. There is no note in it of that poignancy of feeling which we find in David's lament for Jonathan, or in "Tennessee's Pardner"; but the story itself is sufficiently eloquent, eloquent of an ideal of human loyalty which takes friendship rather than love for its supreme expression—seeming indeed to suggest that there is something finer about friendship than love—something, might one say, less selfish, more essentially divine. "Passing the love of woman"! It is to be remembered that that famous phrase was made by a great lover of women, by the lover of Bathsheba, the man who placed Uriah in the front of the battle. David had known both love and friendship, but we say "David and Jonathan"—not David and Bathsheba.

THE TALE OF KING COUSTANS
THE EMPEROR

III

The Tale of King Coustans the Emperor

WHILE no less picturesque than the two romances we have already considered, the Tale of King Coustans the Emperor is perhaps even more important than any of them from the point of view of the literary antiquarian. Its significance in this respect is somewhat fully set out by Mr. Jacobs, with his accustomed learning, in his introduction to William Morris's "Old French Romances." For the fulness of knowledge the reader is referred to Mr. Jacobs. Here it will suffice to hint at one or two points of that antiquarian interest which Mr. Jacob more fully develops.

The story affords a striking illustration of that intercourse between East and West which was brought about by the Crusades, and to which Western thought owed so much of its early quickening. "Permanent bonds of culture," says Mr. Jacobs, "began to be formed between the extreme East and the extreme West of Europe by intermarriage, by commerce, by the admission of the nobles of Byzantium within the orders of chivalry. These ties went on increasing throughout the twelfth century till they culminated at its close with the foundation of the Latin kingdom of Constantinople."

Till this period, of course, Constantinople had retained its ancient name of Byzantium; and our

story has a further historical interest in that it professes to be the legend of how the name was changed.

In the Old French form of the
story, the metrical romance from
which William Morris made his
version, the "Dit de l'empereur
Constant," occur these lines:

> "Pour ce qui si *nobles* estoit,
>   Et que nobles œvres faisoit,
>   L'appielloient *Constant le noble*,
>   Et pour çou ot *Constantinnoble*,
>   Li cytés de Bissence a non"—

which may be freely translated:

> "So noble was he,
>   So noble were his deeds,
>   That men called him Constant the
>   Noble,
>   And from that, Constantinople,
>   The [old] city of Byzantium, takes its
>   name."

We shall come upon still another
etymology in the course of the

story; and we may note that this old romance takes no account of a certain Constantine the Great with whom more official history associates the name of the city.

The story itself may have come as far as from India and reached Constantinople via Arabia and Greece; and the Rev. Sabine Baring - Gould has found it, slightly disguised, so near home as in Yorkshire. You can find it, too, in Grimm under the title of "The Devil with Three Golden Hairs." Perhaps it may interest the reader to compare the Yorkshire version, as told by Mr. Jacobs, with the story as told by William Morris from the Old French. The story is entitled "The Fish and the Ring," and is as follows:

"A girl comes as the unwelcome sixth of the family of a very poor man who

lived under the shadow of York Minster.
A Knight, riding by on the day of her
birth, discovers, by consultation of the
Book of Fate, that she is destined to
marry his son. He offers to adopt her,
and throws her into the River Ouse. A
fisherman saves her, and she is again discovered after many years by the Knight,
who learns what Fate has still in store for
his son. He sends her to his brother at
Scarborough with a fatal letter, ordering
him to put her to death. But on the way
she is seized by a band of robbers, who
read the letter and replace it by one ordering the Baron's son to be married to
her immediately on her arrival. When
the Baron discovers that he has not been
able to evade the decree of fate, he still
persists in her persecution, and taking
a ring from his finger throws it into the
sea, saying that the girl shall never live

with his son till she can show
him that ring. She wanders about
and becomes a scullery-maid at
a great castle, and one day
when the Baron is dining at the
castle, while cleaning a great fish
she finds his ring, and all ends
happily."

With this preliminary note let
us turn to our story:

While Constantinople was still
known under its old name of Byzantium, it was ruled over by a certain Emperor Musselin—known
only, one may add, to romance.
This Musselin was of course a
"paynim," and, ecclesiastically
speaking, a lost soul; but, for all
that, he appears to have been a wise
and much cultivated man; and he
was particularly learned in those

forbidden sciences by which man is
able to read the stars and consult
the devil. After the manner of
Eastern potentates, he was given
to roaming the streets of his city at
nightfall, incognito, and on one occasion being thus out in search of
adventure, accompanied by one of
his knights, he came by a house
wherein was a woman in sore travail of child-bearing. She was a
Christian woman, and as the Emperor and his companion stayed
their steps beneath her window
and hearkened to her cries, they
became aware of her husband
aloft in a high solar praying aloud
to his God in a manner which
caused them much surprise and
speculation.

At one moment he prayed that

she might be delivered, and at another prayed that she might not.

Mystified by this strange prayer, and angered by what seemed to him a lack of chivalry toward a woman in her extremity, the Emperor determined to question the husband.

"So help me Mahoume and Termagaunt!" he swore, "if I do not hang him, if he betake him not to telling me reason wherefore he doeth it!   Come we now unto him."

So they went into the house, and the husband, in no wise recognizing the Emperor, made no concealment of his reasons for his strange prayer. He was, he told, a student of astrology, and watching the stars while his wife was in travail, he perceived, by the signs in the heaven, certain moments when it would be propitious for their child to be born, and certain other moments when for him to be born would mean certain perdition. Therefore, at the propitious moments he prayed to God for his wife to be delivered, and at the unpropitious moments he prayed for her delivery to be stayed; and so well had his knowledge and his prayers availed that, at the moment of the strangers addressing him, a man-child had been born in a good hour.

"How in a good hour?" asked the Emperor; and the man, still unsuspecting, answered that his son was destined to marry the daughter of the Emperor, then eight days old, and that some day he would become lord of the city and emperor of the whole earth.

Concealing his anger at this strange answer, the Emperor privily instructed his knight to carry away the new-born babe and bring it to his palace; and this the knight in no long time was able to accomplish—for the women were so busied arranging the mother that they took no note of the knight as he stole into the room and found the babe lying wrapped in linen upon a chair.

When the Emperor saw the child, he was so filled with hatred of it that he took a knife and slit its breast right down to its navel. He made even to tear out its heart, but the knight begged him to desist, promising to take it away and drown it in the sea.

Now, as the knight carried the babe toward the sea-shore, his heart softened, and instead of drowning it, he left it wrapped in a silken coverlet before the gate of a certain abbey of monks,

who were even then at their ma-
tins.

Presently the monks heard the
child crying, and, going to the gate,
found it there and brought it to
the abbot, who, seeing that it was
a comely child, determined to
nourish and rear it. Having, too,
discovered its wound, he sent for
leeches and demanded of them for
what sum they would heal him.

And here comes in the second
punning etymology of the city of
Constantinople to which I have
previously referred.

The leeches asked a hundred
bezants for their services; but to
this sum the abbot demurred as
excessive, and finally arranged to
pay fourscore bezants. Thereon
he baptized the infant and named

him Coustans, because, he said, "he costed exceeding much for the healing of him."

But, belike, this was merely a pleasantry on the part of the abbot, for he neglected naught that was needed for the child's upbringing. Good nurses he found him, and, when he had reached the age of seven, found him good teachers, so that he was soon learned beyond his years; and when Coustans was some twelve years old, so comely and clever a lad was he that the abbot loved to have him in his sight and would take him to ride abroad with him in his retinue.

Now it chanced that, when Coustans was fifteen, the abbot had some ground of complaint to lay before the Emperor—who was liege-lord of the abbey—and the Emperor having appointed a day for the audience, the abbot appeared before him; and the lad Coustans was in his train.

When the business had been concluded between the abbot and the Emperor, the Emperor noted the handsome boy and asked concerning him. Thereon the abbot told him the story: How the monks had found him at the abbey door some fifteen years ago, and how sorely and in what manner he had been wounded, and how he had been healed and nurtured and schooled at the abbey; and as the Emperor heard the story, he understood that Coustans was the child whom he had wounded years ago and given to his knight to cast into the sea—but of this he made no sign, only communed with himself as to how he might get the boy into his power.

Thus he asked the abbot to give him to him for his own train, and the abbot answered that he must first speak of the matter to his convent, and so went his way.

Now the monks, fearing the wrath of the Emperor, counselled the abbot that the Emperor should have his desire; and thus Coustans was taken to the court and given into the hands of his enemy.

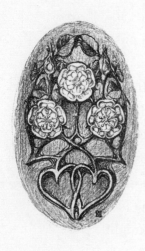

But the Emperor could not for a time devise a means how he might slay the boy; yet soon there were matters arising which took him on a long journey to the borders of his kingdom, and he took Coustans with him. Then, one day when he was still far distant from his capital, he wrote a letter to the burgomaster of Byzantium, and bade Coustans ride night and day till he came to the city. And the letter which the boy carried was on this wise: "I, Emperor of Byzance and Lord of Greece, do

[72]

thee to wit who abidest duly in my
place for the warding of my land;
and so soon as thou seest this letter
thou shalt slay or let slay him who
this letter shall bear to thee, so
soon as he has delivered the said
letter to thee, without longer tar-
rying. As thou holdest dear thine
own proper body, do straightway
my commandment herein."

So Coustans, knowing not that
it was his own death that he carried in his wallet, made such
haste upon his journey that he arrived at Byzantium within fifteen
days.

And here the story goes so pret-
tily in William Morris's version
that it would be unfair to the
reader to attempt another:

"When the lad entered the city

it was the hour of dinner; so, as God would have it, he thought that he would not go his errand at that nick of time, but would tarry till folk had done dinner: and exceeding hot was the weather, as is wont about St. John's-mass. So he entered into the garden all a-horseback. Great and long was the garden; so the lad took the bridle from off his horse and unlaced the saddle-girth, and let him graze; and thereafter he went into the nook of a tree; and full pleasant was the place, so that presently he fell asleep.

"Now so it fell out, that when the fair daughter of the Emperor had eaten, she went into the garden with three of her maidens; and they fell to chasing each other about, as whiles is the wont of maidens to play; until at last the fair Emperor's daughter came under the tree whereas Coustans lay a-sleeping, and he

was all vermeil as the rose. And when
the damsel saw him, she beheld him with
a right good will, and she said to herself,
that never on a day had she seen so fair
a fashion of man. Then she called to her
that one of her fellows in whom she had
the most affiance, and the others she
made to go forth from out of the garden.

"Then the fair Maiden, daughter of
the Emperor, took her fellow by the hand,
and led her to look on the lovely lad
whereas he lay a-sleeping; and she spake
thus: 'Fair fellow, here is a rich treasure.
Lo thou! the most fairest fashion of a
man that ever mine eyes have seen on any
day of my life. And he beareth a letter,
and well I would see what it sayeth.'

"So the two maidens drew nigh to the
lad, and took from him the letter, and
the daughter of the Emperor read the
same; and when she had read it, she fell

a-lamenting full sore, and said to her fellow: 'Certes, here is a great grief!' 'Ha, my Lady!' said the other one, 'tell me what it is.' 'Of a surety,' said the Maiden, 'might I but trow in thee I would do away that sorrow!' 'Ha, Lady,' said she, 'hardily mayest thou trow in me, whereas for naught would I uncover that thing which thou wouldest have hid.'

"Then the Maiden, the daughter of the Emperor, took oath of her according to the paynim law; and thereafter she told her what the letter said; and the damsel answered her: 'Lady, and what wouldest thou do?' 'I will tell thee well,' said the daughter of the Emperor; 'I will put in his pouch another letter, wherein the Em-

peror, my father, biddeth his Burgreve to give me to wife to this fair
child here, and that he make great
feast at the doing of the wedding
unto all the folk of this land;
whereas he is to wot well that the
lad is a high man and a loyal.'

"When the damsel had heard
that, she said that would be good
to do. 'But, Lady, how wilt thou
have the seal of thy father?' 'Full
well,' said the Maiden, 'for my
father delivered to me four pair of
scrolls, sealed of his seal thereon;
he hath written naught therein;
and I will write all that I will.'
'Lady,' said she, 'thou hast said
full well; but do it speedily, and
haste thee ere he awakeneth.' 'So
will I,' said the Maiden.

"Then the fair Maiden, the

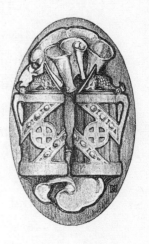

daughter of the Emperor, went to her coffers, and drew thereout one of the said scrolls sealed, which her father had left her, that she might borrow money thereby, if so she would. For ever was the Emperor and his folk in war, whereas he had neighbors right felon, and exceeding mighty, whose land marched upon his. So the Maiden wrote the letter in this wise:

"'I, King Musselin, Emperor of Greece and of Byzance the city, to my Burgreve of Byzance greeting. I command thee that the bearer of this letter ye give to my fair daughter in marriage according to our law; whereas I have heard and wot soothly that he is a high person, and well worthy to have my daughter. And thereto make ye great joy and great feast to all them of my city and of all my land.'

"In such wise wrote and said the letter of the fair daughter of the Emperor; and when she had written the said letter, she went back to the garden, she and her fellow together, and they found that one yet asleep, and they put the letter into his pouch. And they then began to sing and make noise to awaken him. So he awoke anon, and was all astonied at the fair Maiden, the daughter of the Emperor, and the other one her fellow, who came before him; and the fair Maiden, daughter of the Emperor, greeted him; and he greeted her again right debonairly. Then she asked of him what he was, and whither he went; and he said that he bore a letter to the Burgreve, which the Emperor sent by him; and the Maiden said that she would bring him straightway whereas was the Burgreve. Therewith she took him by the hand, and brought him to the palace, where there was much folk, who all rose against the Maiden, as to her who was their Lady."

All went happily as the Princess devised. The Burgreve knowing full well the seal of his lord the Emperor, and, moreover, delighting in the union of so fair a maid with a squire of such noble bearing, put no obstacle in their way. Coustans and the Princess were married, and the old prophecy overheard by the Emperor so many years ago was thus fulfilled, in spite of all his cruel plotting against it. And so happy were the people of Byzantium in the happiness of their Princess, after the manner of such simple folk, that no man worked in the city for the

[80]

space of fifteen days. All was
eating and drinking and making
merry from early morn far into
the night.

News was brought to the Emperor of the rejoicings in his city
and much he marvelled when the
story was told him. But, being a
wise man, he realized that his persecution of Coustans, so long and
so cruelly waged, must as fate de-
creed be fruitless, and so he made
no more fight against an evident
destiny, but peaceably accepted
his son-in-law and showed him
great honor, making him a knight
and heir to all his lands. And so
it befell that on the death of Musselin, Coustans ruled over Byzantium, according to the prophecy,
and under his rule the land be-

came Christian. Many years did he and his wife live in happiness together, and there was born to them a son named Constantine, who became a very great knight and in his turn ruled over Byzantium—from his time onward known as Constantinople, because, as was previously told, of his father Coustans, who, the good abbot had said, had cost so much for his healing.

BLONDE OF OXFORD
AND JEHAN OF DAMMARTIN

IV

Blonde of Oxford and Jehan of Dammartin

THE impoverished nobleman in search of his fortune—or, more strictly speaking, her fortune —is a figure that has met with all too little sympathy. The romance of his position, the excitement of his adventure, have been but little recognized. Far back in the thirteenth century, however, there was a certain trouvère, Philippe de Reimes, of whom nothing is known beyond his name and the two metrical romances that bear it, who saw the poetry and pluck of a gentleman thus essaying to re-

gild the family escutcheon. In his day French noblemen on such a quest made for England, as nowadays English noblemen make for America. England was then, it would appear, the heiress-producing country, and in his moralistic exordium to the charming story he has to tell Philippe de Reimes is very emphatic on the duty of a poor gentleman thus to fare abroad, instead of remaining idle at home, "a burthen to himself and to his relatives who love him." "He of whom I am now going to tell you," he concludes, "was none of these idlers, but he went into a foreign land to gain renown and honor—by seeking honor he arrived at it, and I will tell you how it happened."

All good fairy-tales have morals—to which no one pays the least attention. The moral is like a grace after meat. Philippe de Reimes puts his at the begin-

ning instead of the end, and then proceeds to the real business of his fancy, the
pretty and spirited telling of a story,
which, while it breathes the rose-garden
fragrance we associate with the words
"Old France," is alive too with picturesque and stirring incident and telling
strokes of character—the romantic history of Blonde of Oxford and Jehan of
Dammartin.

Completely to fulfil the requirements
of romance, Jehan should have been a
younger son. As it was, however, he was
the eldest son of a certain aged knight,
renowned for arms in his youth and for
hospitality in his age, whose lands lay at
Dammartin, in the Ile-de-France—acres
broad, but alas! mortgaged by the old
man's youth. A wife much beloved remained to him, with two daughters and
four sons. Now when Jehan arrived at

the age of twenty, he realized the
family situation, and determined
to do what in him lay to repair it.
So, taking a horse, and "twenty
sols" in his pocket, and a "var-
let" to name Robin for his squire
—Robin seems to be a favorite
name for squires in romance—he
set out for England, and, presently
arriving at Dover, found himself
on the high-road to London. On
the way he came up with the retinue of a great lord likewise journeying to London. It was the
Earl of Oxford. Jehan lost no
time in introducing himself, and
telling his story, with the result that
the Earl engaged him as an esquire
of his household. In London
Jehan, as his esquire's duty was,
carved for his master on an occa-

sion when the Earl was dining with
the King, and performed his office
so adroitly that his place in the
Earl's favor was at once secure.
So skilfully, indeed, did Jehan
carve, that when he accompanied
the Earl to Oxford, his graceful
manners winning the Countess at
once, he was appointed to wait at
table upon their only child, the
Lady Blonde. Jehan of Dammartin was a French gentleman of
blood as good, doubtless, as the
Earl of Oxford's, but he did not
disdain to stand before the young
lady of the house and carve for her,
like the humblest servitor. Imagine certain dukes and earls one
could name deferentially perform-
ing the office of waiter for certain
young ladies of the Middle West.

Philippe de Reimes gives us a long floriated troubadourish description of the beauty of Blonde of Oxford, a description running to hundreds of honeysuckle lines, and showing him quite an interesting master of the literary methods of his time.

Now Jehan had carved for his beautiful young mistress for the space of eighteen weeks, without his having paid any attention to the charms so elaborately catalogued by Philippe de Reimes—so occupied was he, it would appear, with his carving. But one night his eyes fell on her with such a fixity of wonder and love that—he forgot his carving. Now for Blonde of Oxford up till this time, and long after, Jehan of Dammartin was nothing more than a servant—with certain gifts, it is true, for musical instruments and parlor games, which, I should

have said, had already made him popular
with everyone in the Earl of Oxford's
house, from Earl to waiting-maid. Therefore, when his eyes forgot his carving for
her face, and his hands lay idly on each
side of the roast, dreamily grasping the
carving knife and fork, she reprimanded
him with the directness of wealthy young
ladies of all times and countries. "Jehan," said she, "carve—you seem beside
yourself!"

Jehan took the rebuke and—carved;
but, next day the same enchantment befell him, and his young mistress rebuked
him even more severely. "Jehan," said
she, "carve. Are you asleep, or are you
adream? If you please, give me something to eat, and leave your dreaming for
the present!"

The rhymes in the old French give a
rather comical piquancy to the reproach:

"Puis li redist: 'Jehan, trenchiés!
Dormés-vous chi, ou vous songiés?
S'il vous plaist, donés m' a mengier;
Ne ne welliés or plus songier."

This time the rebuke so disconcerted poor Jehan that he cut two of his fingers and was obliged temporarily to depute his office to another esquire, and retire to his chamber. There he lay complaining sadly to himself of a wound much deeper and more important than the wound to his fingers; and, presently, to his delighted surprise, his young mistress appeared by his bedside to inquire about his fingers, with, however, nothing more than the conventional solicitude of a mistress. "Jehan," said she, "are you much hurt? Tell me how you are."

"Truly, lady," he replied, "I know not how it happened, but I cut myself to the bone. But it is not this wound that grieves me; I think I have some other disease, for I have lost all my spirits, and have been unable to eat either yesterday or to-day; and I feel a great fainting of the heart, that I hardly know what to do." "Truly, Jehan, I am much concerned at that," said the Lady Blonde courteously; "you must pay attention to your diet, and ask for whatever you like until you are restored." "Lady," said Jehan, "many thanks!" but he added in a whisper between his teeth, "Lady, it is you who carry the key of my life and health, of which I am in such danger."

Blonde, however, did not hear these words, and it was not till Jehan had lain in bed for five weeks, refusing food, and unresponsive alike to the skill of doctors and the kind attentions of the Earl and Countess, that the truth began to dawn upon her. Yet, even so, her suspicion that Jehan's malady was the old malady of love awakened within her as yet no reciprocal sympathy. Her regret for Jehan's illness seems still to have remained regret for Jehan in his capacity as—carver. Yet, it must be admitted that she was prepared to do a great deal to retain the services of a mere serving-man. Jehan must have been a wonderful carver. When, as I have said, he had lain in bed five weeks, and his life was despaired of, the Lady Blonde came once more to his bedside, and besought him to tell her the truth about his illness. "Jehan," said

she, "fair friend, tell me what is the cause
of your being reduced to this condition; I
wish to know, and therefore tell me, and
I pray you by the duty you owe me not
to conceal it from me. I give you my true
word that, if I can find a cure for you, you
shall be no longer ill." "Many thanks,
gentle lady," answered Jehan, "your
words are very sweet; but know that I
see no way by which I can be cured of
this disease; nor have I sufficient courage to venture on saying what is the medicine which would restore me. Nevertheless, there is a medicine by which, if
she who has it in her power would ad-
minister it, I should no doubt be relieved;
but I die from the want of courage to de-
clare it." "Jehan, fair friend," answers
Blonde, "you shall not do that; for, were
you, it would be a great sorrow to me.
Never before have I prayed you for any-

thing, but now I pray this of you for your own good; tell me your malady, and I swear to you on my life that I will labor to cure you, if only I know what ails you." "Will you, lady?" "Yes, truly; now talk to me without fear." "Lady, I dare not." "Nonsense, I will know it one way or other." "If you will, lady, then you shall know it; it is for you that I suffer."

The murder was out, and with the strain of confession Jehan fainted. Blonde brought him back to life with caresses and soothing words. "Friend," said she, "since for my sake you have faced the point of death, I will give you comfort; therefore, put your trust in me, and think only of getting well, and know that as soon

as you are well again you shall be my 'bon ami.'" "Shall I, Lady? Is it truth that you say?" "Yes, friend, be assured of it." "Then, lady, I shall be well again, for I have no other malady." "Eat then, fair, sweet friend, and let your heart be at ease." "Lady, I will do as pleases you; when you will, I will eat."

Now, strange as it may sound, the Lady Blonde was through all this, thinking of Jehan as a carver, and not for a moment as a lover. She feared his dying, because with his death she would lose so dexterous a carver. She pretended otherwise, as we have seen, merely to resuscitate him at table—as poor Jehan soon discovered; for his rapid recovery was to prove a bitter

disappointment. In a night or two he
was carving for Blonde as had been his
custom, but, as he furtively and humbly
stole a glance at her immortal face, he
became aware that she had forgotten all
she had said by his sick-bed—that, in
fact, he was once more a servant.

One day he came upon her in a meadow, weaving a chaplet of flowers, and—
reminded her. Somewhat haughtily and
humorously she looked up at him, and
frankly acknowledged that she had been
thus complacent merely to help him back
to health again. In fact, she had pretended to love him, so that he might rise
from his sick-bed — and carve for her
once more.

Jehan had only to realize this to go
back to bed again, and in a day or two
was so much more ill than before that his
squire Robin aroused the maidens of

Blonde and Jehan

Lady Blonde's bedchamber in the middle of the night with the news that Jehan was dying.

Hastily drawing a "pelicon" of ermine around her—for beautiful ladies in those days went to bed with nothing on—Blonde hurried to Jehan's bedside, and, when she saw how far-spent he was for love of her, love too was suddenly born in her own heart, and, overcome with pity for poor Jehan, and remorse for her past cruelty to him, she fainted away. Presently reviving, she loaded him with caresses and sweet words, so that Jehan, who had hardly been aware of her presence, slowly came back to life. Then she nursed him gently after the manner of fair women and persuaded him to eat some cold chicken "au verjus." And so she stayed with him till daylight, when they parted affianced lovers, and Jehan slept for the first time in eight days. His recovery was now no less rapid than before, and this time the Lady Blonde did not go back on her word, but the two continued to be happy secret lovers for the space of two years—though Philippe de Reimes would have you understand that theirs was a strictly innocent love.

This beatific state of things was suddenly broken in upon by news from France. Jehan's father was ill and had sent over sea for his son. Jehan's grief on hearing this news was great, but it is to be feared that it was not entirely filial in its origin. The Earl and Countess comforted him as best they could, but he had to wait till nightfall to have speech of his

lady. They meet at last in the
moonlit orchard, and seated side
by side under a pear-tree give way
at once to their love and their sorrow. Philippe de Reimes makes a
pretty picture of it.

> *" Beneath a pear-tree beautiful*
> *Jehan and Blonde sit sorrowful;*
> *Weeping sore together they,*
> *Tear-wet cheek on cheek they lay,*
> *In a piteous embrace*
> *Their fair bodies interlace,*
> *For their hearts with grief are full*
> *Beneath that pear-tree beautiful.*
> *Ere they have power to speak, full fain*
> *Five hundred kisses sweet they drain,*
> *And fair and pleasant seemed y-wis*
> *Each unto each such services.*
> * Nor was there any unkissed place,*
> *Nor eyes, nor aught of either face*
> *Left of their lips unvisited;*
> *The while the bitter tears they shed*
> *Their faces sweet have watered.*

The lovers then agree—it was
the Lady Blonde's heavenly sug-

gestion—that, though they must part now, they will meet again on the same night on the following year, under the same pear-tree, and Blonde will fly with Jehan to France. The lark has taken the place of the nightingale and the moon has long since left the orchard before they can find courage to part, and with the morning Jehan and his trusty Robin ride away, accompanied by two palfreys laden with "white sterlings," good silver money of England, the parting gift of the Earl of Oxford, who had taken leave of Jehan in the most affectionate manner. Jehan must return, he had said, and he would make him steward of all his lands. "You shall have the charge of everything, and take what you like," were his words, and Jehan had answered, with a tongue rather saucily addicted to plays upon words, "If it please God, I will return one day, and take something of yours." "In faith," the Earl had innocently answered again, "I am much pleased to hear it."

In due course Jehan reaches his home at Dammartin, and shortly after his arrival his father dies, and Jehan becomes his heir. He goes to Paris to do homage for his lands to the King, and the King is anxious to take him into his service; but Jehan, with his heart in England, has other plans, and his three brothers take his place in the royal household. Jehan, returning to Dammartin, pays his father's debts and generally sets his affairs in order, and then, as the months begin to go by, he makes the mysterious purchases of a choice palfrey, a rich "sambue," or lady's saddle, stuffed with cotton, and a silk bridle. It will soon be time to set out for "le plus bel périer du monde."

Meanwhile, that had happened to the

Lady Blonde which both had feared. Her father had insisted on choosing her a husband, and the bridegroom was to be the Earl of Gloucester. Blonde succeeds in obtaining four months' delay on the plea of mourning for her mother, but not a day longer will her father grant. Now, of course, the four months will be up exactly on the day she has promised to meet Jehan under the pear-tree.

At length the time comes for Jehan to start, and he and Robin and that daintily caparisoned palfrey say good-bye to Dammartin and, reaching the sea-coast, set sail for Dover. On landing there Jehan pays the shipman ten pounds to await his return, and takes the road to London. Arrived in London, he lodges at a fashionable inn, and presently saunters out into the streets to view the town. Soon he comes upon a great crowd of busy people, and, on inquiry, he learns that it is the retinue of the Earl of Gloucester, who is passing through London on his way—to marry the Earl of Oxford's daughter. The marriage had been delayed four months, but the Earl is to marry her, Jehan learns, on the very day of the pear-tree. His heart sinks at the news, but his faithful Robin reassures him, hitting on the right explanation that Blonde had arranged the four months' delay in order to keep her faith with him.

On the morrow, Jehan and the Earl of Gloucester take the Oxford road about the same time, and, the two parties coming up with each other, the Earl, perceiving that Jehan is a Frenchman, addresses him courteously in bad French, asking his name. Jehan answers that his name is Gautier, and that he comes from Montdidier. The Earl makes a rude jest on his name, and then offers to buy the palfrey. Jehan, pretending to be a dealer, affects assent, but asks so large a price for it that the Earl thinks him a fool, and declines the bargain.

Thus they ride on in company and the journey gives Jehan the opportunity for some more of his saucy humor. Toward evening a storm comes on, and the Earl, who is very richly dressed, is wet through, his robe of "green sendal" being ruined. "If I were a rich man as you are," mocks Jehan, "I would always carry a house with me in which I could take shelter; I should not then be soiled, or be wet, as you are."

This remark confirmed the Earl's opinion that Jehan was a fool—like all Frenchmen, for that matter!

Again, later on, they come to a river, which has to be crossed by a ford. The Earl misses the ford, is carried off into the deep water and has to be rescued by fishermen; while Jehan and Robin cross over dry-shod. "If I had such a multitude of followers," was Jehan's sarcastic comment, "I would always carry a bridge with me, so that I could pass every river with ease."

This remark hugely tickled the Earl and his followers, who once more laughed heartily at Jehan for a fool. Nevertheless, the Earl seems to have been taken with Jehan, and, as they near Oxford, invites the further pleasure of his society.

But Jehan replies that his way takes him through a by-road, as near there he had once seen a fair hawk for which he had laid a snare, and he must now go to see if it is caught. Once more the Earl is convinced of his folly, for by this time surely, he laughs, net and bird, if caught, will both be rotten. And with this final sally, the Earl goes his way and Jehan his.

Meanwhile, the castle of Oxford is all a-hum with guests awaiting the coming of the Earl, and Blonde is awaiting the night and the coming of Jehan. She seems to have had no misgivings, but as night falls, contriving to steal away from her relatives, she packs her jewels into a casket, and

[108]

takes her stand under the pear-
tree with perfect confidence—the
most beautiful pear-tree in the
world!

As we know, her faith was not
in vain, and she has not long to
wait before Jehan appears, punc-
tual to the second, to take into his
arms that "something" of the
Earl of Oxford's he had promised
to steal. After the first customary
transports, the lovers waste no
more time in caresses, but soon
the white palfrey is carrying its
delicious burden on the way to
France, and Jehan and Robin are
keeping a sharp look-out for danger. They avoid the highway and
take their course through by-path
and woodland, travelling by night
and resting by day, and a very

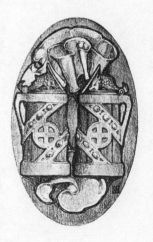

pretty journey they make of it. The indispensable Robin looks after the larder. While the lovers lie hidden in the depths of the forest he repairs to the nearest town and comes back laden with cakes, white bread, and pasties of capons, not to mention "wine in two barrels."

> "*Robin loads his horse's pack,*
> *To those lovers carries back*
> *Capon pasties and white bread*
> *To the place where they are hid;*
> *And wine there was, for barrels two*
> *Went ever with those lovers true.*
> *Upon the green grass then they spread*
> *A napkin fair embroideréd,*
> *And eat beneath the branching boughs.*
> *Close at hand their horses browse,*
> *And Robin every need supplies*
> *With his ever watchful eyes.*
> *When on pasties and white bread*
> *The happy lovers thus are fed,*
> *In each other's arms all day*
> *They kiss and talk the time away;*
> *Much and sweet they had to say.*
> *And the woods with them rejoice,*
> *All the greenness, the sweet noise*
> *Of nightingale and mavis call,*

[110]

And the other birdies small
That sweetly in their wildwood Latin
Woodland vesper sing and matin.
Naught these lovers doth annoy,
Hearing is enough of joy,
And with other such delights
Pass their happy days and nights."

Meanwhile, of course, things had been happening in the castle of Oxford. On his arrival, the Earl of Gloucester had been anxious to see his young wife without delay, and Blonde had been sent for. Not being found, her father had at first assumed that she had hidden herself away for some mysteries of the feminine toilet, in order to make herself especially beautiful for her bridegroom, and, while they awaited her, the Earl of Gloucester filled in the time by anecdotes of the 'good fool' of a Frenchman, a droll fellow, whom he had met on the way. As he talked, there was something about the anecdotes that irresistibly

[111]

reminded the Earl of Oxford of
Jehan, and, the Lady Blonde
continuing to be missing, her
father came to the conclusion
that the Earl's fellow-traveller had
indeed been Jehan of Dammartin, who had come to keep his word
and carry off that "something"
that was his. He confided his
fears to the Earl of Gloucester,
with the result that the Earl immediately sets off in pursuit of
the poor lovers, with a great company of men-at-arms, thunder-
ing along the highways toward
Dover.

But, of course, Jehan had not
overlooked this danger, and when
at last his little cavalcade is in
sight of the sea, he hides with
Blonde in a forest, and sends out

Robin in disguise to reconnoitre.
Robin finds all the roads senti-
nelled by the Earl's retainers, and
the boat which was faithfully
awaiting them watched by four
men-at-arms. But he contrives to
get speech of the shipman, whom
he finds loyal, and arranges with
him the details of the desperate
embarkation they are to attempt
that midnight. The shipman's
heart is with the lovers, and there
are twenty stout lads on his ship
to lend a hand. So night comes
and Jehan and the white palfrey
and Robin steal softly out of the
woods toward the, unfortunately,
moonlit strand. The Earl's
watchers are on the alert, and
immediately attack them. As
there are but four of them, how-

ever, it is an easy matter for Jehan
to dispose of three. But the fourth
has time to blow a horn which brings
the Earl and his retinue immediately
upon the scene. Then follows a
spirited piece of fighting which shows
Philippe de Reimes as a poet of vigor as
well as of nightingales:

> "la douce noise
> Des mauvis et des roussignos."

Need one say that, in spite of the Earl's
superior forces, Love was too strong for
him? Unhorsed by Jehan, he lay dan-
gerously wounded on the sand, half his
retainers dead and the rest in panic; and
so at last the white palfrey may delicately
step aboard and the sails fill out for Bou-
logne and Dammartin.

The rest of the story is just—happy
ending. Surely no reader will need to be
told how the King of France bestirred

himself on behalf of the two lovers and won for them the not difficult forgiveness of the Earl of Oxford, who had always had a weakness for Jehan; how the Earl made a splendid visit to Dammartin, how honors were heaped upon Jehan, how Blonde bore him four children, "the most beautiful in the world," and how, when his father-in-law died, Jehan became Earl of Oxford as well as Count of Dammartin, and how Jehan lived to enjoy all this good fortune for thirty years.

So fate blesses a true love and honors it—sometimes.

The reader's prayers are requested for the repose of Philippe de Rheims, whose soul, it is to be hoped, is long since in Paradise:

> Pour cou n' oblierai-ge mie
> Que je ne vous pri et requier
> Que vous vœlliés à Dieu priier

Que Phelippe de Reim gart
Et de paradis li douist part.*

* The writer is indebted for this story
to the complete text, edited by M. LeRoux
de Lincy, and published by the Camden
Society.

AUCASSIN AND NICOLETE

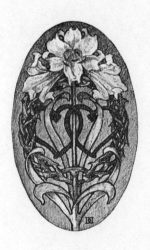

V

Aucassin and Nicolete *

THOUGH the song-story—"cante-
fable"—"C'est d'Aucassin et de
Nicolete," has long had an antiquarian
interest for scholars, it is only during
the last twenty years or so that it has
taken its place in the living literature of
the world, and given two of the most fra-
grant names to the mythology of lovers.

Monsieur Bida in France, and Mr.
Andrew Lang and Mr. F. W. Bour-

* Although this sketch of Aucassin and Nicolete was embodied in the companion volume to
this, "Old Love Stories Retold," it is nevertheless
so typical a romance of Old France, that I have
ventured to reprint it here in its more accurate
classification.

dillon in England, are to be
thanked for rescuing this precious
pearl from the dust-heaps of phil-
ological learning. In England Mr.
Bourdillon was first with a very
graceful and scholarly translation.
Walter Pater in his famous essays
on "The Renaissance" early di-
rected to it the attention of ama-
teurs of such literary delicacies;
but practically Mr. Lang is its
sponsor in English, by virtue of a
translation which for freshness and
grace and tender beauty may well
take the place of the original with
those of us for whom Old French
has its difficulties. Nine years before, Mr. Edmund Clarence Stedman had introduced the lovers to
American readers in "A Masque
of Poets." There in a single lyric

Mr. Stedman has so skilfully con-
centrated the romance of the old
story that I venture to quote from
it, particularly as Mr. Stedman
has done readers of his poetry the
mysterious unkindness of omitting
it from his collected poems:

"Within the garden of Biaucaire
  He met her by a secret stair,—
  The night was centuries ago.
  Said Aucassin, 'My love, my pet,
  These old confessors vex me so!
  They threaten all the pains of hell
  Unless I give you up, ma belle,'—
  Said Aucassin to Nicolette.

"'Now, who should there in heaven be
  To fill your place, ma très-douce mie?
  To reach that spot I little care!
  There all the droning priests are met;—
  All the old cripples, too, are there
  That unto shrines and altars cling,
  To filch the Peter-pence we bring';—
  Said Aucassin to Nicolette.

. . . .

"'To purgatory I would go
  With pleasant comrades whom we know,

[121]

Fair scholars, minstrels, lusty knights
Whose deeds the land will not forget,
The captains of a hundred fights,
The men of valor and degree:
We'll join that gallant company,'—
Said Aucassin to Nicolette.

.　　.　　.　　.　　.　　.　　.

"'Sweet players on the cithern strings
And they who roam the world like kings
Are gathered there, so blithe and free!
Pardie! I'd join them now, my pet,
If you went also, ma douce mie!
The joys of heaven I'd forego
To have you with me there below,'—
Said Aucassin to Nicolette."

Here the three notes of the old song
story are admirably struck: the force and
freshness of young passion, the troubadourish sweetness of literary manner, the
rebellious humanity. Young love has
ever been impatient of the middle-aged
wisdom of the world, and fiercely re-
sisted the pious or practical restraints to
its happiness; but perhaps the rebellious-
ness of young hearts has never been so

audaciously expressed as in "Aucassin
and Nicolete." The absurdity of parents,
who, after all these generations of ex-
perience, still confidently oppose themselves to that omnipotent passion which
Holy Writ itself tells us many waters
cannot quench; the absurdity of thin-
blooded, chilly old maids of both sexes
who would have us believe that this
warm-hearted ecstasy is an evil thing, and
that prayer and fasting are better worth
doing—not in the most "pagan" literature of our own time have these twin ab-
surdities been assailed with more out-
spoken contempt than in this naïve old
romance of the thirteenth century. The
Count Bougars de Valence is at war with
Count Garin de Biaucaire. The town
of Biaucaire is closely besieged and its
Count is in despair, for he is an old man,
and his son Aucassin, who should take

his place, is so overtaken with a hopeless passion that he sits in a lovesick dream, refusing to put on his armor or to take any part in the defence of the town. His father reproaches him, and how absolutely of our own day rings his half-bored, half-impatient answer. "'Father,' said Aucassin, 'I marvel that you will be speaking. Never may God give me aught of my desire if I be made knight, or mount my horse, or face stour and battle wherein knights smite and are smitten again, unless thou give me Nicolete, my true love, that I love so well. . . .'"

Father—*can't* you understand? How strange old people are! Don't you see how it is?

"Father, I marvel that you will

be speaking!" It is the eternal ex-
clamation, the universal shrug, of
youth confronted by "these te-
dious old fools!"

Now Nicolete is no proper
match for Aucassin, a great
Count's son—though, naturally,
in Aucassin's opinion, "if she were
Empress of Constantinople or of
Germany, or Queen of France or
England, it were little enough for
her"—because she is "the slave
girl" of the Count's own Captain-
at-arms, who had bought her of the
Saracens, reared, christened and
adopted her as his "daughter-in-
God." Actually she is the daughter of the King of Carthage, though
no one in Biaucaire, not even herself, knows of her high birth. The
reader, of course, would naturally

guess as much, for no polite jongleur of the Middle Ages, addressing, as he did, an audience of the highest rank, would admit into his stories any but heroes and heroines with the finest connections.

Father and son by turns have an interview with the Captain. The Captain promises the Count to send Nicolete into a far country, and the story goes in Biaucaire that she is lost, or made away with by the order of the Count. The Captain, however, having an affection for his adopted daughter, and being a rich man, secretes her high up in "a rich palace with a garden in face of it." To him comes Aucassin asking for news of his lady. The Captain, with whose dilemma it is possible for any one not in his first youth to sympathize, lectures Aucassin not unkindly after the prescribed formulas. It is impossible for Aucassin to marry Nico-

lete, and were he less honest, hell would
be his portion and Paradise closed against
him forever. It is in answer to this
admirable common sense that Aucassin
flashes out his famous defiance. "Paradise!" he laughs—"in Paradise what
have I to win? Therein I seek not to enter, but only to have Nicolete, my sweet
lady that I love so well. For into Paradise go none but such folk as I shall tell
thee now: Thither go these same old
priests, and halt old men and maimed,
who all day and night cower continually
before the altars and in the crypts; and
such folk as wear old amices and old
clouted frocks, and naked folk and shoe-
less, and covered with sores, perishing of
hunger and thirst, and of cold, and of
little ease. These be they that go into
Paradise; with them have I naught to
make. But into hell would I fain go; for

into hell fare the goodly clerks, and goodly knights that fall in tourneys and great wars, and stout men-at-arms, and all men noble. With these would I liefly go. And thither pass the sweet ladies and courteous that have two lovers, or three, and their lords also thereto. Thither go the gold, and the silver, and cloth of vair, and cloth of gris, and harpers, and makers, and the princes of this world. With these I would gladly go, let me but have with me Nicolete, my sweetest lady."

Aucassin's defiance of priests as well as parents is something more significant than the impulsive utterance of wilful youth. It is at once, as Pater has pointed out, illustrative of that humanistic re-

volt against the ideals of Christian
asceticism which even in the Middle Ages was already beginning—
a revolt openly acknowledged in
the so-called Renaissance, and a
revolt growingly characteristic of
our own time. The gospel of the
Joy of Life is no mere heresy
to-day. Rather it may be said
to be the prevailing faith. Aucassin's spirited speech is no longer
a lonely protest. It has become a
creed.

Finding Aucassin unshaken in
his determination, the Count his
father bribes him with a promise
that, if he will take the field, he
shall be permitted to see Nicolete
—"even so long," Aucassin stipu-
lates, "that I may have of her two
words or three, and one kiss."

[129]

The compact made, Aucassin does so
mightily "with his hands" against the
enemy that he raises the siege and takes
prisoner the Count Bougars de Valence.
But the father refuses the agreed reward
—and here, after the charming manner
of the old story-teller himself, we may
leave prose awhile and continue the story
in verse—the correct formula is "Here
one singeth:"

"When the Count Garin doth know
   That his child would ne'er forego
   Love of her that loved him so,
   Nicolete, the bright of brow,
   In a dungeon deep below
   Childe Aucassin did he throw.
   Even there the Childe must dwell
   In a dun-walled marble cell.
   There he waileth in his woe,
   Crying thus as ye shall know:
' Nicolete, thou lily white,
   My sweet lady, bright of brow,
   Sweeter than the grape art thou,
   Sweeter than sack posset good
   In a cup of maple wood . . .

"My sweet lady, lily white,
  Sweet thy footfall, sweet thine eyes,
  And the mirth of thy replies.

"'Sweet thy laughter, sweet thy face,
  Sweet thy lips and sweet thy brow,
  And the touch of thy embrace.
  Who but doth in thee delight?
  I for love of thee am bound
  In this dungeon underground,
  All for loving thee must lie
  Here where loud on thee I cry,
  Here for loving thee must die,
    For thee, my love.'"

Now Nicolete is no less whole-hearted
and indomitable in her love than Aucassin. She is like a prophecy of Rosalind
in her adventurous, full-blooded girlhood.
When her master has locked her up in the
tower, she loses no time in making a vig-
orous escape by that ladder of knotted
bedclothes without which romance could
hardly have gone on existing. Who that
has read it can forget the picture of her
as she slips down into the moonlit garden,

and kilts up her kirtle "because of
the dew that she saw lying deep
on the grass"?—

"Her locks were yellow and
curled, her eyes blue and smiling,
her face featly fashioned, the nose
high and fairly set, the lips more
red than cherry or rose in time
of summer, her teeth white and
small; her breasts so firm that
they bore up the folds of her bod-
ice as they had been two apples;
so slim she was in the waist that
your two hands might have clipped
her, and the daisy flowers that
brake beneath her as she went
tiptoe, and that bent above her
instep, seemed black against her
feet, so white was the maiden."

As Nicolete steals in the moon-
light to the ruinous tower where

her lover lies, she hears him
"wailing within, and making dole
and lament for the sweet lady he
loves so well." The lovers snatch
a perilous talk, while the town's
guards pass down the street with
drawn swords seeking Nicolete,
but not remarking her crouched
in the shadow of the tower. How
Nicolete makes good her escape
into the wildwood and builds a
bower of woven boughs with her
own hands, and how Aucassin
finds her there, and the joy they
have, and their wandering together
in strange lands, their losing each
other once more, and their final
happy finding of each other again
—"by God's will who loveth lovers"—is not all this written in the
Book of Love?—

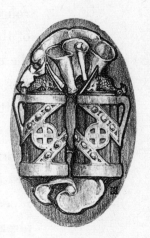

"Sweet the song, the story sweet.
  There is no man hearkens it,
  No man living 'neath the sun
  So outwearied, so foredone,
  Sick and woful, worn and sad,
  But is healèd, but is glad,
    'Tis so sweet."

The story is simple enough, of a pattern old and familiar as love itself, but the telling of it is a rare achievement of art, that art which is so accomplished as to be able to imitate simplicity; for, roughly connected as are certain parts of the story, "Aucassin and Nicolete" in the main is evidently the work of one who was a true poet and an exquisite literary craftsman. The curious, almost unique form of it is one of its most characteristic charms; for it is written alternately in prose and verse. The verse sometimes repeats in a condensed form what has already been related in the prose, sometimes elaborates upon it, and sometimes carries on the story independently. The formula with which the prose is introduced is: "So say they, speak they, tell they the Tale," and the formula for introducing the verse, as already noted, is: "Here one singeth." These formulas, and the fact that the music for some of the songs has come down to us on the precious unique manuscript preserved in the Bibliothêque Nationale, lead critics to think that the romance was probably presented by a company of jongleurs, with music, and possibly with some dramatic action. The author is unknown, and the only reference to him is his own in the opening song:

> "Who would list to the good lay,
> Gladness of the captive gray?"

M. Gaston Paris suggests that the "viel caitif" lived and wrote in the time of Louis VII. (1130), and Mr. Lang draws a pretty picture of the "elderly, nameless minstrel strolling with his viol and his singing-boys . . . from castle to castle in 'the happy poplar land.'" Beaucaire is better known nowadays for its ancient fair than for its lovers. According to tradition, that fair has been held annually for something like a thousand years—and our lovers have been dead almost as long. Still, thanks to the young heart of that unknown old troubadour, their love is as fresh as a may-bush in his songs, the dew is still on the moonlit daisies where Nicolete's white feet have just passed, and her bower in the wildwood is as green as the day she wove it out of boughs and flowers. As another old poet has

[136]

sung, "the world might find the
spring by following her"—so ex-
quisitely vernal is the spirit that
breathes from this old song story.
To read in it is to take the advice given to Aucassin by a certain knight. "Aucassin," said the
knight, "of that sickness of thine
have I been sick, and good coun-
sel will I give thee: . . . mount thy
horse, and go take thy pastime in
yonder forest; there wilt thou see
the good flowers and grass, and
hear the sweet birds sing. Per-
chance thou shalt hear some word,
whereby thou shalt be the better."

The reader will do well to take
the knight's advice, and follow
into the woodland "the fair white
feet of Nicolete."

[NOTE: The reader may care to compare Walter Pater's translation of the

description of Nicolete with Mr. Lang's given on page 139: "Her hair was yellow in small curls, her smiling eyes blue-green, her face clear and feat, the little lips very red, the teeth small and white; and the daisies which she crushed in passing, holding her skirt high behind and before, looked dark against her feet; the girl was so white!"]

THE HISTORY OF OVER SEA

VI

The History of Over Sea

ONE of the great charms of mediæval story is the romantic indefiniteness of the geography, as also its sublime independence of formal historical events. As we have seen in the tale of King Coustans, the story-teller is in no wise abashed by the discrepancies between his version of the origin of Constantinople and the version of the official historians. Anachronism has no terrors for him, and you can believe him or not as you please. Of course, you prefer to believe

him. Similarly the events of the mediæval story-teller take place in countries for
which you will look in vain on the map,
but he were dull, indeed, and hard to
please, who would demand the latitude
and longitude of such realms of old
romance as Belmarye and Aumarie.
Such a one might at the same time demand an exact localization of the Forest
of Arden or the Woods of Broceliande.
Even places that are to be found on
earthly maps take on a certain mythical
unreality from the romantic atmosphere;
and such places as Acre and Joppa, for
example, seem rather to belong to dream-
land than to geography.

The scene of "The History of Over
Sea" is situated partly in "Aumarie,"
ruled over by that potentate of romance
known as "the Soudan"—how much
more suggestive than "Sultan"—and

partly in an old France hardly less mythical. It opens in "Ponthieu," which once upon a time was ruled over by a certain Count of Ponthieu, a very valiant and good knight. In his near neighborhood lived another great lord, the Count of St. Pol. Now Count St. Pol had no son, so his nephew Thibault, son of his sister, Dame of Dontmart in Ponthieu, was his heir. The Count of Ponthieu had one fair daughter, whose name the chronicler does not deem it necessary to give, she being a mere woman; and by a second wife he had a son, and both son and daughter he loved much. Now my Lord of Thibault, though heir to his uncle, was a poor man, and must needs work for his living, as only gentlemen could work in those days, with his lance and sword. Therefore, having won the approval of the Count of Ponthieu, he became one of the knights of his retinue, and rode with him to tournaments; and in these and other warlike expeditions he did so valiantly and profitably for his master that the Count was highly pleased with him. One day as they returned together from a tournament, the Count called him to his side and said:

"'Thibault, as God may help thee, tell me what jewel of my land thou lovest the best.'"

"'Sir,' answered Thibault, 'I am but a poor man, but as God may help me, of all the jewels of thy land I love none so much as my damosel, thy daughter.'"

The Count, when he heard that, was much merry and joyful in his heart, and said: "'Thibault,

I will give her to thee if she will.'"
"'Sir,' said he, 'much great thanks
have thou; God reward thee.'"

Then went the Count to his
daughter, and said to her: "'Fair
daughter, I have married thee,
save by thee be any hindrance.'
'Sir,' said she, 'unto whom?' 'A
—God's name,' said he, 'to a much
valiant man, of much avail: to a
knight of mine who hath to name
Thibault of Dontmart.' 'Ha, sir,'
said she, 'if thy country were a
kingdom, and should come to me
all wholly, forsooth I should hold
me right well wedded in him.'
'Daughter,' said the Count, 'bless-
ed be thine heart, and the hour
wherein thou wert born.'"

So all is well, and my Lord
Thibault and the Count's daugh-

ter are married, and live happily together for five years. They had but one
sorrow. "It pleased not our Lord Jesus
Christ that they should have an heir of
their flesh, which was a heavy matter to
them."

One night as Thibault lay by the side
of his sleeping wife, he pondered much
on this sorrow of theirs, and why it
should be, seeing that they loved each
other so well, and the thought came to
him of "St. Jakeme, the Apostle of Ga-
licia," who was said to befriend such as
were thus denied the gift of children.
Presently his wife awoke, and taking her
in his arms he begged a gift of her.
"'Sir,' said the dame, 'and what gift?'
'Dame,' said he, 'thou shalt wot that
when I have it.' 'Sir,' she said, 'if I may
give it, I will give it, whatso it may be.'
'Dame,' said he, 'I crave leave of thee

to go to my lord St. Jacque the Apostle,
that he may pray our Lord Jesus Christ
to give us an heir of our flesh, whereby
God may be served in this world, and
the Holy Church refreshed.' 'Sir,' said
the dame, 'the gift is full courteous, and
much debonairly will I grant it thee.'"

A night or two after, as they were
again lying side by side, the wife speaks.
"'Sir,' said she, 'I pray and require of
thee a gift.' 'Dame,' said he, 'ask, and
I will give it, if give it I may.' 'Sir,' she
said, 'I crave leave of thee to go with
thee on thy journey.'"

Thibault was sorrowful to hear this,
and said: "'Dame, grievous thing would
it be to thine heart, for the way is much
longsome, and the land is much strange
and much diverse.' She said: 'Sir, doubt
thou naught of me, for of such littlest
squire that thou hast shalt thou be more

hindered than of me.' 'Dame,' said he, 'A—God's name, I grant it thee.'"

So it was arranged, and in no great while Thibault and his wife start out on their pilgrimage, the Count of Ponthieu having smiled upon their departure, and bestowed upon them "pennies" for their journey. At first all goes well with them on the road, and at length they come to a town within two days' journey of the saint. Here they put up for the night, and on the morrow, asking the landlord concerning the way they should take and the condition of the roads, he makes a fair report, and once more they start out with a good heart. After journeying for some time they come to a forest,

and presently find themselves at a
parting of the ways. There are
two roads, one to all appearance
good, and one bad, and they know
not which to take. Thibault, his
wife, and chamberlain, have rid-
den ahead of the retinue, and, the
place seeming lonesome and threat-
ening, Thibault sends back his
chamberlain to bring up his servants. Meanwhile, further exam-
ining the roads, he decides to take
the good one, not suspecting that
certain forest thieves thus made
the bad road seem good as a trap
for unwary travellers. For the
space of a quarter of a league the
road continued broad, but suddenly it grew narrower, and ob-
structed with low-hanging boughs;
and Thibault turned to his wife

with misgiving: "'Dame,' said he, 'me-seemeth that we go not well.'"

The words had scarcely left his lips, than there came in sight four stout fellows mounted on four great horses, and each rider held a spear in his hand. Turning to look behind him, Thibault is aware of four others similarly mounted and armed, and presently one of the first four rides at him with drawn sword. Thibault, who is unarmed, contrives to evade the stroke, and also to snatch the sword from the robber's grasp. With it, by God's help, he is able to slay three of the eight thieves, but the combat is too un-equal, and presently he is overpowered and stripped of his raiment. The thieves then bind him hand and foot with a sword-belt and cast him into a bramble-bush. Turning then to his lady, they take and strip her in like manner even

unto her smock, and then fall to dis-
puting among themselves as to whose
prize she shall be.

"'Masters,' said one of them to his
fellows, 'I have lost my brother in this
stour, therefore will I have this Lady in
atonement thereof.' Another said: 'But
I also, I have lost my cousin-german;
therefore I claim as much as thou herein; yea, and another such right have I.'
And even in such wise said the third and
the fourth and the fifth; but at last said
one: 'In the holding of this Lady ye
have no great getting or gain; so let us
lead her into the forest here, and do our
will on her, and then set her on the road
again and let her go.' So did they even
as they devised, and set her on the road
again."

Meanwhile, Thibault, lying in the
bramble-bush, had seen all that befell

in agony of soul, and here comes in
a curious side-light on the position
of woman in the middle ages. It
would not occur to us to-day that
Thibault's dame could be held re-
sponsible for what had happened
to her, and indeed Thibault readily
allows that it was all against her
will and gives her his assurance
that he will not hold it in any way
against her; but he does so with
an evident sense of his peculiar
magnanimity, an evident feeling
that all husbands would not have
been so lenient. His wife, beside
herself with the anguish of her
humiliation, very evidently expected no such clemency, and
indeed is unable to believe that
her lord really means what he
says. So when he calls to her to

release him from his bands, she, spying a sword left behind from the combat, takes it in her hand, and, distraught as she is with shame and fear of her husband, endeavors to smite instead of releasing him. The stroke, however, misses him, and severs the thongs, so that he springs to his feet, and, taking the sword from her, says: "'Dame, so please God, no more to-day shalt thou slay me;' to which she humbly answers: 'Of a surety, sir, I am heavy thereof.'" Thibault seems to bear her no ill-will for her action, but, laying his hand on her shoulder, he leads her back along the road till they meet his retinue, by whom they are soon provided with changes of raiment, and fresh

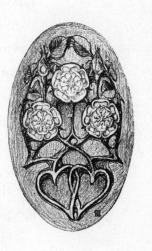

[153]

horses, and so once more continue their
way to St. Jakeme, or St. Jacque. At the
next town Thibault leaves his wife in the
care of some good sisters, and proceeds
toward the saint alone. His pilgrimage
accomplished to his satisfaction, he re-
turns for his Lady, and both take the
home journey together for Ponthieu, he,
says the old story-teller, evidently feeling
it a matter for emphasis, treating her
"with as much great honor as he had led
her away, save the lying a-bed with her."

During the day of festivity which sig-
nalized their return home, the Count of
Ponthieu and his son-in-law sat together
at table, familiarly eating from one dish;
and presently the Count asked Thibault
to tell him for his entertainment some
tale from his travels, either some expe-
rience of his own, or some of which he
had heard. Thibault at first professed

ignorance of any such story to tell, but,
on the Count's continuing to urge him,
he withdrew him away from the rest of
the company and proceeded to tell his
own story, though without revealing the
identity of the persons involved. When
the story was ended, the Count asked
Thibault what the knight had done with
the lady, and the conversation which
ensues gives lurid evidence that, after
all, Thibault was an exceptional husband for those days. He gave answer
to the Count that "the knight had
brought and led the Lady back to her
own country, with as much great joy
and as much great honor as he had
led her thence, save lying in the bed
whereas lay the lady."

"'Thibault,' said the Count, 'otherwise deemed the knight than I had
deemed; for by the faith which I owe

unto God, and unto thee, whom much I love, I would have hung the Lady by the tresses to a tree or to a bush or by the very girdle if none other cord I might find.'

"'Sir,' said Messire Thibault, 'naught so certain is the thing as it will be if the Lady shall bear witness thereto with her very body.'"

Other times, other manners, indeed! No one seems to give a thought to the shameful suffering of the Lady herself. It would seem as though the crime had been committed entirely against the husband and the father. The Count now grows curious as to the name of the knight, and, though Thibault endeavors to dissuade him, will not be gain-

[156]

said. His persistence breaks down
Thibault's resolution and at last
he tells the full truth. But the
Count's savage sense of justice
is by no means weakened by the
shame being thus brought so
near home. "Much grieving and
abashed, he held his peace a great
while, and spake no word; and
when he spoke he said: 'Thibault, then to my daughter it was
that this adventure betid?' 'Sir,'
said he, 'of a verity.' 'Thibault,'
said the Count, 'well shalt thou be
avenged, since thou hast brought
her back to me.'

"And because of the great ire
which the Count had, he called
for his daughter, and asked her if
that were true which Messire Thibault had said; and she asked

'What?' and he answered: 'This, that thou wouldst have slain him, even as he hath told it?' 'Sir,' she said, 'yea.' 'And wherefore,' said the Count, 'wouldst thou have done it?' 'Sir,' said she, 'hereto, for that it grieveth me that I did it not; and that I slew him not!'"

To say the least, Dame Thibault's answer was hardly politic at the moment, and may perhaps set one thinking that the mediæval husband cannot be judged by our mild modern conditions. After all, when a wife expresses her regret in cold blood that she had not murdered her husband, we can hardly be surprised if that husband hangs her by her hair to the next tree. But the Count of Ponthieu, albeit he was her father, was planning for her a still more terrible punishment.

We next find him at a little seaport

which the story-teller familiarly refers to as "Rue-on-Sea," as if there were any such place, and his daughter, his son and his son-in-law are with him there. The Count is there on grim business. First, he has made for him an immense barrel, very strong and thick, and having shipped this on board a stout craft, he bids his daughter and his son and Thibault come aboard with him, and thereon they are rowed out to sea, none save the Count knowing the meaning of their trip. When they had gone some two leagues, the Count smote off the head of the barrel, and paying no heed to her frenzied entreaties or those of her companions, he compelled his daughter to get into the barrel. Then, replacing the staves and having made all water-tight, he thrust the barrel over the boat's side into the sea, saying, "I commend

thee unto the winds and waves."
So had Perseus and his mother
Danæ been cast adrift by the
angry king centuries ago, and, as
even a heathen providence had
taken pity upon a weak woman in
a like extremity, it was not to be
thought that in Christian times
such distress should go unsuc-
cored; "but our Lord Jesus
Christ, who willeth not the death
of sinners—be they he or she,"
quaintly remarks the pious story-
teller, "but that they may turn
from their sins and live, sent
succor unto the Lady."

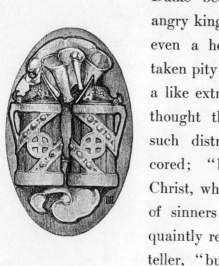

It chanced that a short while
after the Lady Thibault had thus
been commended unto the winds
and the waves, a merchant ship
outward bound from Flanders

passed by where the great barrel
was rolling to and fro upon the
waters. Being espied by one of
the merchants, it was hauled on
board, and great was the astonish-
ment of the voyagers on discovering its strange cargo. The poor
Lady was far spent with lack of
air, but the ministrations of her
rescuers soon brought her to herself, and "she ate and drank and
became much fair." So fair, indeed, did she seem in the sight of
the merchantmen, that, when at
length they arrived at "Aumarie,"
it occurred to them that they might
turn her beauty to good account
with the Soudan, who, like all
Soudans before and since, was a
lover of fair women. So, attiring
her in fair apparel, they brought

her as a gift to the Soudan, who was a
young man and as yet unwed. The
Soudan, who was noble and gentle of
nature, treated her with great distinction,
but in vain asked her to reveal her name
and people. However, he perceived her
to be of high lineage, and, being captivated
with her beauty, begged her to renounce
her religion and become his wife. Real-
izing that her only hope of escape was
through his love, the Lady Thibault con-
sented, and, having recanted Christianity,
she became the Soudan's wife according
to the laws of the Saracens, and she and
her Saracen husband appear to have lived
very peacefully together; for as a husband
the Soudan seems to compare most favor-
ably with the Christian Thibault. In due
course, and with appropriate rejoicings, a
son is born to them, and again a daughter,
and the years begin to go by.

Meanwhile, the conscience of the Count of Ponthieu grows more and more troublesome for the crime committed in his anger against his daughter, and her husband and brother are likewise haunted with the thought of her. At length the Count confesses his sin to the Archbishop of Rheims, and his son-in-law and his son alike make confession, and all three take the vow of pilgrimage Over Sea, that is, to the Holy Land. Presently setting out on their journey, they arrive over sea, and having visited all the shrines and holy places, they give themselves to the service of the Temple at Jerusalem for the space of a year. Thus having eased their souls, they bethink them once more of this world and Ponthieu, and presently take ship at Acre on their homeward voyage. At first the winds and the waves, to which

[163]

the Count had commended his
daughter are favorable, but one
day a storm arises, and their only
hope from shipwreck is to take
refuge in the land of Aumarie, in
spite of the risk they thus run at
the hands of the heathen Saracens.
However, a deferred death by
martyrdom seems preferable to im-
mediate death in the sea, so they
make for the nearest port in Aumarie. As they run in towards
shore, they are boarded by a
Saracen galley, and taken prison-
ers, and their captors, as they had
foreseen, made a present of them
to the Soudan, captured Christians
being a particularly ingratiating
gift to Saracen monarchs. The
Soudan had them cast into dif-
ferent prisons, with heavy chains

and little food, and generally they were treated with much hardship. And so they abode in prison many days, knowing nothing of their nearness to the Lady Thibault, she being no less ignorant of them. At length the Soudan's birthday came round, and as the custom was, the people came to him and demanded their yearly right—"a captive Christian to set up at the butts." The Soudan granted them their request as a matter of course. "'Go ye to the gaol,' said he, 'and take him who has the least of life in him.'" On going to the gaol, the Count of Ponthieu, emaciated, and with matted hair and beard, seemed to have little enough life in him to serve their purpose, so when they brought him before the Soudan

he bid them take the old man away and
do their will upon him. But as the
Soudan's lady, sitting by the side of her
lord, looked on the poor captive, something stirred in her heart, and it was as
though her very blood told her who the
captive was, though her eyes had not
recognized him. So turning to the Soudan she said: "'Sir, I am French, wherefore I would willingly speak to yonder
poor man before he dieth, if it please
thee.' 'Yea, dame,' said the Soudan,
'it pleases me well.'" Coming to the
captive, the lady Thibault asked him of
what land he was and what kin and he
answered sorrowfully: "'Lady, I am of
the Kingdom of France, of a land which
is called Ponthieu; and certes, dame, it
may not import to me of what kin I be,
for I have suffered so many pains and
griefs since I departed that I love better

to die than to live; but so much can I
tell thee of a sooth, that I was the Count
of Ponthieu.'"

When his daughter hears this, without revealing her identity, which the old
Count had not suspected, she goes to her
lord, the Soudan, saying: "'Sir, give me
this captive, if it please thee, for he
knoweth the chess and the tables, and
fair tales withal, which shall please thee
much; and he shall play before thee and
learn thee.' 'Dame,' said the Soudan,
'by my law, wot that with a good will
I give him thee; so do with him as thou
wilt.'"

The jailers then led out Thibault, and
again his wife asks for speech with him,
and again begs him of the Soudan,
and again her request is granted. Her
brother is then brought out, with the
same result. He too knows the chess

and the tables! "'Dame, said the indulgent Soudan, 'by my law, were there an hundred of them I would give them unto thee willingly.'" What is a captive Christian more or less! So the Lady Thibault's kindred thus pass into her safekeeping, and the populace are just as much pleased with another Christian prisoner, who, unfortunately not being acquainted with the Soudan's lady, passes duly to his martyrdom.

The Soudan's lady then proceeds to nurse and nourish her captives, sore wasted with their stay in prison, and provides them with fitting raiment, so that at length they are restored, and daily play at the chess and the tables before her, and the Soudan himself takes pleasure in their company. But, all this time, the dame wisely refrains from discovering herself. Now, after some time has gone by, a neighboring Soudan goes to war with the Soudan of Aumarie, and herein the Soudan's lady sees an opportunity of escape. Going to her kinsmen, she asks them still more particularly about themselves and their histories, ending with: "'And thy daughter, whom this knight had, what became of her?'"

"'Lady,' said the Count, 'I trow that she be dead.' 'What wise died she?' quoth she. 'Certes, Lady,' said the Count, 'by an occasion which she had deserved.' 'And what was the occasion?'" said the lady.

The Count then related the whole history, and when he comes to where his daughter raised the sword against her husband, the wife of the Soudan exclaims: "'Ha! sir! thou sayest the sooth; and well I know wherefore she would to do it.' 'Dame,' said the Count, 'and wherefore?' 'Certes,' quoth she, 'for the great shame which had befallen her.'"

Thibault then protests with tears that he would not have held her blameworthy. "'Sir, that she deemed naught,'" answered the Lady. Then she falls to questioning them as to whether they think the Count's daughter alive or dead. "'Dame, we wot not,' they answer. 'But if it pleased God,' she continued, 'that she were alive, and that ye might have of her true tidings, what would ye say thereto?'"

All protest that to see her alive again
would be better than to be out of prison,
better than to be King of France, better
than to be endowed with all the riches
of the world; and softened with these
answers, she at length reveals herself,
and unfolds her plans for their escape
to Ponthieu. First Thibault must ac-
company the Soudan in battle, and trust
to winning his good-will by his valor,
and this part of the plan is accomplished
with such brilliant success to the Soudan's arms that Thibault is at once set
high in his favor. He offers Thibault
wide lands and a rich wife, if only he
will become a Saracen. The Soudan's
Lady temporizes for him, and meanwhile,
falling ill, informs her lord that she is
with child, and that she has been warned
that she will die if she is not presently
taken to some other soil away from

the city. The ever-indulgent Soudan, for whom one begins to feel
sorry, immediately falls in with his
wife's wishes, and has a ship prepared for her that she may voyage
to whatever land she deems good—
so simple as well as gentle was the
redoubtable Soudan of Aumarie.
His Lady begs to take her old and
young captives for her entertainment, cunningly proposing to leave
Thibault behind. The Soudan
grants this request also, but demurs
to her leaving Thibault. So brave
a warrior will be a great protection
for her on her voyage, he says.
So presently all four are aboard,
and she has taken with her also
the Soudan's little son—which
seems hardly fair. And now,
"'if God please, we shall yet be

[172]

in France and the land of Ponthieu.'"

After a while the mariners come
to a port on the French coast,
another seaport in the moon,
called "Brandis." Here is the
good land where the Lady would
be set down, and once safely on
land with her companions she
turns to the mariners. "'Masters',
she says, 'get ye back and tell to
the Soudan that I have taken from
him my body, and his son whom
he loved much, and that I have
cast forth from prison my father,
my husband, and my brother.'"
With this message the mariners
must needs return disconsolately
to Aumarie; and the moral of the
story, when you come to reflect
that her Christian kinsmen had

set her adrift in a barrel, and her "paynim" lord had ever been a gentle loving
husband, is, to say the least, cynical and
hardly calculated to encourage Saracen
potentates in clemency towards Christian
captives.

However, these happy people of Ponthieu appear to have given little thought
to the feelings of the Soudan, but as
soon as possible repair to Rome, where
"the Apostle" sets the Lady Thibault
"in right Christendom" once more, and
thence to Ponthieu, and a future filled
with "great joy" and "great pleasure,"
and all manner of good fortune and
honors.

Incidentally, it must be told that the
Lady Thibault's daughter by the Soudan
whom she had left behind in Aumarie,
and who was known as the Fair Caitif,
grew up passing fair, and, being given

in marriage to the famous Turk, "Mala-
kin," became through him the grand-
mother of the great Saladin. So, at all
events, says the old romancer.

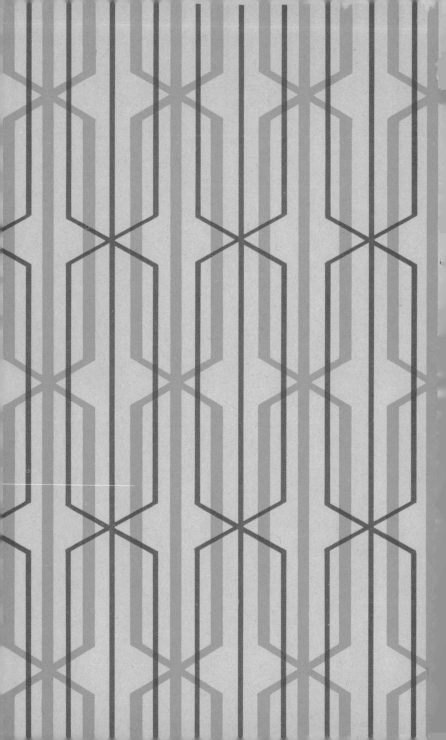